KANE

When it's to good to be true

ASHLEY LEE

Table of Contents

The Best Part

CHAPTER 1

Kane and I have been dating for about ten months. He is, in my opinion anyway, the epitome of the most perfect man. Beautiful white teeth, great hygiene, stellar credit, no kids, nor has he been married, intelligent, successful, respectful, God-fearing, and the list goes on! We met in Texas where I had lived my entire life. But due to Kane's flexibility and wealth, it seemed like Texas would soon be in the past.

I fantasized about living my days like a royal queen. Flying in jets, eating breakfast in Hollywood while I watch the sunset in Hawaii that same night. Though we had only started talking barely months before, Kane always made me feel and look so wonderful and it was better than I ever imagined.

"Are you almost ready, my love?" Kane asked, snapping me out of my daydreaming.

"Yes baby, give me about 10 minutes". I rushed to apply the last touches of my makeup and throw on my Louboutin heels.

Our bags had already been transported from the room to the jet. We were about to settle in for a long 13-hour trip to Japan. Kane did a lot of business overseas and he maintained a special bond with the people of Japan. It became one of my favorite spots. Since meeting Kane I've been to over thirty different countries and have so many passports I stopped paying attention.

My life before Kane, you could say, was less than rewarding. Not that I didn't have anything going on, but I was not where I wanted to be, or where most people my age would be comfortable being, depending on past living experiences, I guess! I was what you could call a "struggling entrepreneur". I didn't believe in the traditional 9-5 stuck-forever-in-life type of lifestyle so I had my fingers in multiple MLM companies trying to make it work best as I could. And a struggle it was. I always wondered how Kane worked his magic so smooth and effortlessly as if it had never been a problem or a thought. It was always a complete turn on for me to watch a man work, especially when he's confident and good at what he does. It seemed as if he thoroughly enjoyed me getting excited at the sight of him being professional. Any chance we got when he wasn't busy, I was busy doing him.

I sat across from him on the ostrich and alligator stitched seats. The scent of lemongrass and salted caramel invaded my nostrils, instantly putting me in a relaxed and hungry mood. I was beginning to think about all the delicious meals I wanted to enjoy. It made me look over at Kane who was sprawled out on his reclined chair wearing his hoodie and sweats. He dressed a bit more comfortably because of the length of the trip and because he had the luxury of bathing and dressing while we were flying over the ocean if he chose. Being around Kane turned me into a bougie bitch quick. That's all he knew anyway. The best or nothing. As I watched him lie back with the daily paper in his hands, I conjured up a few sexual thoughts of where and how I wanted him to explode on me.

We were both in our late twenties with no kids, but he always pulled out. Sometimes it would make me wonder if he was lying about not already having kids, if he thought I wasn't the one, if I was just an on-board booty call, or if he was scared and nervous at the idea of making a family. Besides, he had it more than going on and maybe he wanted to enjoy bachelor living a bit longer. I know I was never in a rush for having children. Being with a man like him will definitely change your opinions about anything you ever thought. Anything I did with Kane was almost life changing. I was in a constant state of excitement not ever worrying about if he'd leave or find someone else, which he may have, but my mother always told me to be careful what I wish for, so I tended to not put those thoughts into existence.

I finally decided I would make him cum on my mouth and chest while standing over me on the penthouse terrace before I would relax him with a comforting massage. "Did you know that I love you" he stated, from behind his newspaper. I quickly got up, with a grin and sat on his lap. "Is that so". I tried not to be so flattered about his comments and compliments but no woman on this earth could resist! I kissed him across his forehead down to his ear as my legs began to make circles around his groin. He tried to continue on with his reading, but I could hear low groans deep in his throat. His shaft began to bulge, and his 11" magic stick was about to put on a show.

CHAPTER 2

The past ten months have been an unexpected bliss for me since I met Olivia in Texas. It was another routine board meeting at Donna Channel. The largest company out of the five I own. Donna Channel is a custom diamond/ jewelry store for the prominent and elitist. Starting price for any diamond or piece of jewelry was a solid $250,000. It wasn't my first business, but it definitely brought in the most revenue. Partly because diamonds aren't only a woman's best friend. Turns out that cats, dogs, and other "pets" can turn them into a showpiece as well.

I like to keep my meetings brief but mostly informative. I prefer to hear feedback from my team than to give demands and instructions. They know exactly how the company goes about its business, so I keep it to a minimum. I always like to be hands-on in activities and show my face, interacting with my workers and promoting through my commercials. It all helps me to keep a good clean image.

The next main event for Donna Channel would be held in Japan at a special event called Oiwai. It is hosted for Japanese royals, politicians, and other famous influencers, twice a year. I love going to Japan. It could be from being part Japanese along with black. Even though I am not looked at as a Japanese person among the people, because of my mixed background, they always treated me with much respect and always welcomed me in as family. I absolutely love the culture and the authentic food.

I got a ton of my discipline training here from a local fish market owner named Hoshi, who turned out to be the son of the president of Ayako University. One of the best universities in Japan. Hoshi was the most disciplined person I knew right along with his father. Once I witnessed Hoshi and his father waking up everyday for 3 weeks straight at 3 a.m. to manually stack bricks to build a wall three miles long, just so their animals could be enclosed and for more privacy. All due to his mother not wanting a gated fence and requesting it be done her way. When I noticed the type of discipline and concentration it took to do something so tedious, I knew I wanted to learn something from them.

Hoshi was a mentor to many due to his experiences and his views on life. He always attended my events and would invite the most beautiful Japanese woman to accompany him. Besides my mother deciding to move to Japan, Hoshi was another good reason to visit. As I'm usually the person showing and giving people new experiences and outlooks, Hoshi was that person for me.

As I drank my double shot espresso exiting out of my building and onto Washington Street, I caught a glimpse of her. Olivia James. She had been kneeling in a forest green tight-fitting dress attempting to fix a strap on her matching heels. Little did she know. Green is my favorite color! I waited for the cars to pass before crossing the street to catch up to her. "Excuse me ma'am, there seems to be something wrong with my phone. Could you call it for me to see if it rings!?" I asked playfully. She burst into laughter. Then I realized how silly I just made myself look. But at least someone got a good laugh out of it. I felt a bit at ease knowing that she had a sense of humor. "I didn't envision being approached by someone like yourself with a corny twelve-year-old's pick-up line." she said with a chuckle. I smiled back. But her comment had me wondering if she may have already known who I was. "So, you ran across the street with a corny joke to get my number?" looking at me with question marks in her eyes. "Well, that is a part of the reason, but I wouldn't stop there. My name is Kane and it's a pleasure to meet you, Miss...." hissing along with the Sss until she filled in the blank.

"James. Olivia James" she said extending her hand to shake mine. "What brings you downtown this lovely morning?" I asked. Even though I may be a very professional-looking man, I am still just that. A man! So, as I listened to her speak about her downtown rendezvous, I had already begun to see myself rubbing my hands on her thighs while caressing my fingers through her naturally curly brown hair. I don't just run up on random women on the streets and trust me, there's no need to. But there are times I get instant thoughts and feelings on certain things I should do without much thought. And this was one of them.

"I'm well-traveled and move around quite often for work but it's still a vacation to me. Traveling is a luxury even if it is for work purposes. It's a learning experience so it's always fun. I'm very blessed for it. Two of my favorite destinations are Japan and Bosnia. People there are great plus I have good friends who are from there. How about yourself?" We had been slowly strolling and had just stopped in front of her building. "I absolutely love Miami. The views, beaches, weather, yachts, parties, and sunsets are a few but major reasons for me to continue to visit" she spoke in her heavenly voice with a slight British accent. "There's something I've been wanting to do there while at the beach one night. Guess I'll have to say it's a bucket list idea". "Well I wish we had more time for you to share your idea with me. Sounds like it'll be a good one". "If only you knew". She looked up at me with a seductive glance. "Thank you for your company and humor, Kane". I had whipped out my business card for Donna Channel and handed it to her. As she examined the card before sliding it inside her bra, she smiled and stated that she'd call me later that afternoon so I could tell her something from my bucket list. The only idea on my list was meeting with Miss James again to indulge in her beauty and hopefully, making her more.

CHAPTER 3

There must have been at least 1200 people in attendance at Oiwai. Lights and bright flashing colors illuminated the sky as they announced the top 10 donors to Japanese Charities and other organizations. Top charity donor went to Mr. Wong and his wife for donating over 100 million dollars to their favorite organization that assists homeless families with housing. An organization Kane also did business with. One thing the wealthy loved along with their money, was recognition. They always bask in the glory of being the best and living in the limelight of their work. But I guess that's understandable. Donna Channel was one of the many companies at the venue the wealthy love to indulge in after their small talk and congratulatory Pats on the Back. Buying expensive diamonds and eating exotic foods along with purchasing beautiful foreign cars and animals such as: camels, elephants, eagles, cheetahs, peacocks, gorillas, and kangaroos along with your assortment of sea creatures as well. Rare species of sharks, fish, stingrays and others I have never seen before. I always wondered what people with money spent it on. And the answer is... Anything. Mostly items and ideas you wouldn't even think to buy or try. When you have money, not even the sky is the limit. They have no limit. Saying the sky is the limit would still be limiting them. That's why they secretly venture to outer space without anyone knowing. These types of people do things the average person would believe is unbelievable and absurd. That's what I thought until Kane took me on a 25,000-foot underwater excursion. It takes the cake on being the most extreme activity I've ever done and will ever do. Most people think being in the sky above

25,000 feet is scary but try doing that in the opposite direction. This was something exciting he always wanted to do. A bucket list activity. I had excused myself to the ladies' room to freshen up when I noticed Kane's university professor approach us. He is a well-known honest man renowned for a few of his speeches. As I walked away, I felt Kane's hand slide down and playfully pinch my butt. It startled me but woke me up to the idea of smuggling him into a secret room for some secret fun. I love that Kane was still willing to take risks like that at times, just for the excitement. After that adrenaline rush, I was sure I was going to need to wipe. More so because I never really had panties on. Nothing would have been comfortable with the gown I had worn. Panties only get in the way. I find them useful only during that time of the month.

As I found my way through the crowd and back to Kane, he had finished his talk with his professor and was finishing up another with Hoshi. He had Miss Japan on his arm today. " Nice to see you again Miss James" he said. Both of them with big smiles. Kane and Hoshi hugged and shook hands, then he left.

I followed Kane's lead as he escorted me to where his main setup was located. Once we arrived, we were then shown to another secluded area where there was a hidden door. Kane opened it as I walked in the dark room and he closed the door behind us. Kane walked up behind me and covered my eyes with his hands. "I know something you don't know" he said, keeping his hands over my eyes. Being anxious and growing excited I rubbed my back side against him while my hair caressed his face. "I love surprises, but I hate waiting for them". As he uncovered my eyes, it felt as if a red carpet unfurled to unveil three tables, full of jewelry pieces and very unique diamond cuts. I said nothing. For a moment I was speechless. Before I could say anything, Kane guided me and stopped me in front of one of the tables that was arranged with chocolate and colored diamonds, stones, and pearls.

He gently took my hand and slid on the biggest and most beautiful garnet ring that completely matched my birthstone and my style. He continued to slide on another 16 carat VVS1 diamond on my pointer finger. He then began to take my other hand and slid on a custom-made blue diamond ring with a matching bracelet that had our initials engraved on it along with the date we met. I was sporting at least 3 million dollars in jewelry, not to mention the necklace and earrings I already had on. I felt like the Queen of England. He was definitely letting me know I was the queen in his world.

"Please, enjoy these". I wanted to snatch him up and do him right then on the table, but I had to keep my composure. I walked over to him backing him into a corner while I devoured his lips. There was no use in getting too rowdy here, for I knew we would be leaving shortly. "I wish there were more powerful words than Thank You to express how I feel". "I love you, would do just fine for me babe" he said, gazing into my eyes. "I'm actually okay with your silence". He pulled me in close and whispered in my ear, "The only thing I want to hear next from you… is that sexy curvy ass slapping against my dick in a couple of hours". The way Kane spoke to me, especially sexually, turned me into a slave! I felt like a robot. But I enjoyed everything he programmed me to do.

CHAPTER 4

I awoke to enjoy the scene of Olivia in the kitchen, making what smelled to be even better than what I normally have my staff make for me. Food, for the most part, always smells good while being cooked. But this aroma was clearly from someone who knew a thing or two about satisfying a hungry belly. I've not had a woman cook for me, let alone one that knew how to really throw down. Watching Olivia in the kitchen was giving me morning wood. I had to do something about it, or it would only get worse for me. She had been whisking eggs and chopping vegetables for the omelet she was preparing. Already on the plates were freshly made Texas-sized stuffed French toast, bacon, sausage, and sliced fruit in a bowl. I grabbed a cherry and a strawberry and slowly approached her, rubbing my wood against her voluptuous body. She had on a yellow lace bodysuit showing off just enough skin. I prefer a woman to wear something even if it's just a pair of socks. It still leaves me a small window for my imagination to run wild, before I take it off myself.

I placed the cherry in front of her lips while she made small circles with her tongue around it. She put it in her mouth and seductively ate it then turned around to face me. She had bed head, but her curly hair made her the most beautiful sight. Her nipples were perky and erect and she tip-toed, pushing them against my chest. I took my strawberry and placed it in my mouth hoping that she would take the bait. And she did. She began to lick around my lips as she gently took a bite from the other end. As she began to press her tongue in my mouth it only made me hungry. Looking at my banana pudding appetizer, I grabbed her forcefully by the waist and placed her on the counter. That was something we both loved. She went crazy for my hardcore sexual demands and I loved how submissive she would make herself to me. I loved the role-playing, maybe more than her. She softly moaned, closing her eyes and leaning her head back while I kissed her neck and shoulders, all while my fingers made circles putting a little pressure on her clit. I could feel the moisture behind the lace. I went down to her thighs spreading her legs, putting her feet partially on the edge of the counter. I kissed her on her play area smelling her flowing juices. I began to use my pointer and middle finger to move her lingerie and used my other hand to gently open those lips I've been wanting to kiss for the past 10 minutes! I moved my tongue up and down and side to side. I playfully sucked and watch her nearly jump off the counter as I slowly inserted, not my finger, but a cucumber. Using food for sex, even unusual shapes, can also be used for excitement. Call me a super freak but it floats my boat!

I enjoyed my breakfast of champions then proceeded to wash up for the second part of my meal. Everything on the plate was cooked perfectly and looked as if it had been prepared by my chef. This impressed me. Of all the skills and talents a woman can have, I believe cooking is the best and most important. It is an art, if done right. And my stomach was in a museum of tasteful deliciousness.

CHAPTER 5

We spent a week in Japan exploring new places and purchasing a few goods to bring back to the states with us. My favorite find was a set of samurai swords sold to us by an older couple that had been holding on to it since WW2. It originally was not for sale due to its fragility, value, and sentimental meaning to them, but money talks. As we finished our evening shopping, Kane told me he would take me to see something I've not seen before. We ended up on a secluded black sand beach that was soft on our toes and had little gold sparkles in it. We sat and drank two bottles of wine and spoke of our lives and his next business ventures and how blessed we were to be here. I couldn't help but to envision one of my wildest fantasies, or you could say, my bucket list idea. That was, to utterly and completely enjoy each other on the beach, but that wouldn't happen here. I knew when the right time and place would be, and the time would present itself soon.

It was a beautiful intimate and romantic setting off the coast. We both gazed at a full dark orange moon swirled between blue and purple clouds with hot and light pink tips and edges. A sunset that would make anyone stop and look. "We should go to Miami soon. We've traveled to so many places, but we have yet to go there" I said a tad bit tipsy. "When's the last time you've been?" I asked him. He looked at me and smiled. "Five years ago". "What!" I screamed surprisingly. "Five years! Why so long? As much as you get around, I would have thought you frequented Miami and loved going there". He chuckled. "Well, I think of going at times and it's a beautiful place but when you can travel to other destinations around the world with much more history and even better beaches and amazing sunsets then it doesn't stay a place of interest for long. At least not for me. I've found a few diamonds in the rough and I prefer to choose those over the hype of what people love about Miami. It doesn't have a special meaning to me yet". "Yet", I said again, knowing that the next time he left from Miami it would be a place of great interest. "You know what, I've got one more surprise for you. Unfortunately, you'll have to wait for that", but secretly I didn't care. Everyday was a surprise for me. We walked for a moment down the shore before returning back to our penthouse.

I jumped into the jacuzzi to unwind with a glass of wine while Kane attended to a few phone calls. I reminisced about when I first met Kane and all the trouble I went through trying to get my life together.

I still had two of my internet marketing businesses going so I was still making progress and with the help and resources Kane provided, I was able to really launch myself off the ground. It doesn't always take money to make money but when you're talking about big bucks, it does. Or it could be just knowing the right people. I thanked God for whatever the reason may be for our encounter, knowing it had definitely turned out to be for the better.

I marinated in the warmth for almost an hour before hopping out to fix my hair into a bouquet of beautiful curly locks. I put on my workout leggings and bra for 30-minutes of yoga poses and stretches while listening to soft jazz. I didn't know how long Kane would be before coming to bed, so I got myself wrapped up and into the soft blankets. As I scrolled through the different TV programs, I immediately stopped on one channel when I noticed Kane's face. They were airing his commercial for the organization that assisted with homeless families. In the commercial, Kane was shown handing keys to different families and smiling along with them. He had the smile of an angel. He was wearing a gray suit with a green tie, looking like money. Watching him move swiftly across the screen put a smile on my face. I thought about phoning my best friend, Ava to tell her about my best life these past couple of days but my phone was too far away to reach without me having to move from my comfortable position. I felt the urge to tell someone about how strongly my feelings shifted towards Kane these past few days and how I knew he was the guy I ultimately wanted to share my life with.

I went into thinking how awkward it would be for me to pop the question to him. I'm sure that would be a huge shocker for us both. I wondered how many women may have pushed themselves upon him with no success. I didn't want to turn him off and become another one of his statistics. How often is it that a woman proposes to a man? Do men even find that attractive or wish for things like that? Maybe for a few but was Kane one of those men? I never felt offended or intimidated by anyone in his presence and he always stood by me, so I did not think too much in that direction. Maybe he was planning something special for the right time. Perhaps, he was waiting for me to make that move. That theory didn't last long with me knowing the type of assertive person I know he can be, but sometimes it's those individuals that like to have the opposite role played out in their personal lives. My mind started racing at 100 miles per hour on different ideas of us getting married and popping the question: who, what, when, where, why... and it wasn't long after, that I trailed off to sleep.

CHAPTER 6

This past week in Japan was a very productive and successful one, boosting my sales and putting an extra 2.5 million dollars in my pocket. I had a lot to focus on: hosting events, meeting with CEOs and executives for market expansions and new commercial promotions. All coming up in the next month. I organized my week to begin with commercial prepping and speaking at a few seminars and private parties. I mostly enjoyed the private parties. I've met a lot of great and important people at some of these places and have heard valuable information at them. This is where most of the fun happens. Wealthy people have the most fun because they can do whatever their hearts desire. Only here will you see the most famous and prominent people completely let loose and be themselves.

The second day in Japan I met with Saki Yaki. Saki is a good friend of my mother's. She used to bring us Sukiyaki late nights after she closed her restaurant. A simple dish that has a sweet and salty flavor a little bit like teriyaki, but with beef and vegetables in the mix. It has its own sukiyaki taste people love so much. It was one of my favorite dishes. She was also one of the vice-presidents on the board for the Association of Homeless Families in Japan. She had wanted me to come by her house and have a talk with her grandson Kaito, who she said needed some discipline training and insight. Because he was only ten and looked up to me it was easier for me to get through to him. She says a great mind develops early in life and he should have good people around him so he will develop good habits and become something great, like an emperor! Saki dreamt really big for him.

Kaito and I would have positive chats and I would sometimes let him sit in on different meetings with me. He would turn into a little brother. He was well-behaved so I never minded having him around much. He would take in everything like a sponge, so I was careful of what I exposed him to. He reminded me of myself in ways, at least the good parts.

I had a lengthy talk with Saki about Kaito, her restaurant ,and how I would like to have improvements made to the homeless shelters and housing as well as doing a bit more for a few rejected families. After I got off the phone, I made another call to my mother. She lived alone in her old neighborhood where she mostly grew up. My father passed away six years ago in a tragic work accident. He used to work as a licensed inspection contractor for commercial buildings. One day on the job he was pushed off the side of the building and was impaled by the wires 16 stories below. It was a major blow to my mother and I because we were always a close family.

Since then, my mother has isolated herself in pictures, memories, and lots of shopping and I have pushed myself completely into work. Talking to my mother was always refreshing and sparked energy in me. It was something Olivia was bringing back into me as well. My mother and I never spoke much about my father's passing, but we deeply shared the pain. I tried to put her at ease by telling her to go back home to visit her family and that I'll be okay alone, but she would refuse. Until two years later she finally got tired of being alone and decided to move back to Japan with her sisters. Afterwards, she began to slowly come back to life but would never fully recover. She was a great woman that raised a genius, so she deserved the best. Olivia also deserved the best. No one could fill the hole left by my father, but Olivia occupied a space in my heart that had not been touched or filled before. A space that made the loss of my father feel easier to get through. She gave me even more confidence and support and she always brought out the sexual beast in me.

The simple thoughts of Olivia took me to a happy place where I could lose myself. As my thoughts turned, I pictured her standing in front of me with her warm smile, bouncy curly hair and succulent lips that were always ready to be kissed. I thought of how life-changing it would be to officially make her mine, but something about the thought of marriage did scare me a bit and it changed my view of losing someone close and special when my farther passed but I knew it was something to be cherished. We were headed back to the States, but before we were completely at home, I would surprise her with a stop in Miami. I wanted to find out what all the hype was about to her, and how it would be something I would like to remember. Before long, Miami would be on my special destinations list.

CHAPTER 7

As we entered the beginning of the white flowing beaches of Miami, Kane picked me up with his strong bulging arms as I leaned into his chest and caressed his head with my breasts all over his face! I wanted him to lay me down by the water so I could spread my legs, open wide, so the sand and flowing juices of my pussy, so wet, so pink, so lightly hairy and smooth could lightly tingle with the feeling of wanting to fuck Kane all over. He came down to where my thighs were and kissed softly until his tongue made it to where my sensitive clit was, as his long curvy tongue slithered all over my walls and into my juicy hole. His fingers made it to where his tongue was, as I moved up and down, loving every minute of his licking session.

Slowly I turned around as I put my soft ass in his face as he spread my cheeks and forced his tongue through! It was feeling so good it was time for him to feel on the same level. "Get your ass up! Come shove your hard dick in my mouth, Now!" Quickly, he moved his body towards my face as his cock hit the inside of my warm mouth. Saliva flowed out of my mouth and all down his huge balls! I slurped every drop off his firm cock as I went faster and sucked harder as I felt his dick move inside my mouth. I knew Kane was enjoying it and there was more to come!

Being so strong and sexy, Kane began to pick me up, upside down sixty-nine style as he stood. Ass in face, Dick in mouth! I wanted him to tease me a bit, so I made him suck on my luscious toes till my dripping juices formed a small puddle. "You're so fucking good with your tongue baby. You always know what to do to get me going." As we explored each others' private parts, a couple walked by and decided to enjoy the scene. This made us both excited! The thought of someone watching him screw my brains out turned me on to another level. He put me down as I stood up with my legs opened in a V while he came behind and bent me over. His dick was so big it had to be forced through my love tunnel to gain entrance.

"Oooh...Damn! I like that daddy, do it harder." I couldn't stop moaning as I knew the by-standers were loving every shadow they could catch of us and all the low fading groans they heard with the water splashing away at my feet.

We then proceeded to walk to a single chair where I laid him down and decided to tease him! I gave Kane the sexiest lap dance he ever experienced and by the look on his face and his rock-hard penis I knew I was doing my job right! I shook my pink wetness directly at him as his pointer and middle finger made their way back to my juicy flowing lips as he put his fingers in his mouth and tasted it. I gently sat down on top of him as I turned around bouncing my breasts, while my hard nipples slapped Kane in the face. He smiled and moved his hands from my arms, down my back and around the curve of my ass cheeks as he leaned me forward and started to pound my ass! "Yes, Yes!" I screamed aloud not caring who else was noticing. I could feel the white juiciness of me flowing down my inner thighs as he slapped my booty harder and louder each time. I could feel myself squeeze around his shaft as he squirmed around in the chair letting me know his explosion was near. But it was a bit too soon, so I hopped off and just as fast started to lick him around the tip so the tingle wouldn't go away! "I want you to nut all in my mouth, all over my face, I'm demanding you to bust a big one."

I stroked him for about five minutes until he pulled me up for some more pussy munching. Sixty-nine it was as we both went at it some more. Suddenly, he got very tight, as I got loose. We both were in sync with one another because we both let go! Thick white nut from his bulging dick laid all in my hair, my eyes, my mouth, my finger, the chair and a few feet away in the sand! My nectar laid all over Kane's face like a milk mustache! Like a kid who wanted to be big and strong he made sure to drink up all the good protein I made for him.

"Yum!" I wanted more but now it was time to rest a bit. I laid down on his chest as we cleaned each other off and listened to the calm waves of the beach hit the shore. This was definitely the best part of my day and soon, it would be round two!

The Next Part

CHAPTER 1

Get up baby" I said to Kane who had his legs wrapped around me like a pretzel. "No. I'm not getting up yet, just five more minutes, please" he said with a smirk, as he laid with his head half buried under the pillows. "All right, I'll just fart on you right here" I said with a chuckle, knowing he was going to jump up as if he just saw a spider. "I knew that would do the trick" I said with laughter.

I hopped out of bed to turn the water on for my shower and started playing some Corinne Bailey Rae to deepen my mood. As I entered the shower, the hot water teased my body, giving me goose bumps on my arms and legs. I fully engulfed myself under the shower head and began to massage my hair.

I enjoy being in hot water. It seems to soothe all of my aches and pains I have at the moment, so I always take long showers and baths. I got my morning fresh body wash and began to exfoliate myself with my loofah.

As I bent to wash my legs and toes, I felt the slap of Kane's hand on my wet ass. I could feel the imprint of his hand on my cheek. Before I could get up and balance myself, Kane had already begun to rub himself between my legs. I had to throw my arms up to catch myself, but Kane only saw it as an invitation to continue. "You look fantastic from this view" he said, as he continued to rub himself around my thighs. "Stay just like that".

Kane slowly but firmly inserted the tip of his dick inside me. He began to go deeper as he slowly rubbed his thumb around my other hole. I pushed myself back against him, feeling the water splash on my back and watching the soap bubbles slide down my legs. I raised up on my tip-toes to give myself better balance as I threw my ass up and around his piece. I felt myself cum as he hit my G-spot over and over.

He pulled himself away and examined the quickie work he just put in. He grabbed my loofah and washed my backside and touched me softly. Once again, Kane had me in a trance. I felt that there was nothing I could do at times to control myself in his presence and sexuality.

He finished washing me and himself off then got out of the shower as I stayed in to wash my hair. Not even the best cup of coffee could have started my day off so well. There's nothing like some good shower sex in the morning or just sex period.

: : :

I was beginning to have withdrawals when I wasn't around Olivia for more than a few hours. All I did between meetings and outings was think of her. I would have to go the next week without her around. She had business of her own to handle at home. I would be in Paris working on a masterpiece of artwork I had begun right before I met Olivia but hadn't yet invested the time to go back and complete.

Since I have two events planned in Paris, I would find time in between to work on my new art skills. It was something my mentor Hoshi introduced me to and indulged in himself. I was going to start on something new and present it to Olivia. I planned to ask her to marry me and I wanted to make sure it was done in the right way, so I wanted to get away to clearly think about my options and choices. We kissed each other and said our good-byes before I boarded my jet and was off high in the clouds to France.

CHAPTER 2

As I touched down in Paris, I was greeted by Hoshi and his new fling. We both landed within minutes of each other and were both staying at La Maître Resort, even though we both have real estate here. We got into our shared limo and spoke of politics and had small talk on the way to our hotel. Once I got to my suite, I took in a few glasses of bourbon and phoned Olivia to let her know I was okay and was about to prepare for my upcoming event. She was excited that she had just sealed an important deal with a large premium dealership group that would purchase extended warranties and roadside assistance for all of their pre-owned inventory under her downline. It was a start to great success and residual income. She was going to celebrate and have a night out with her girl Ava.

"It looks like your mentoring is paying off" she said. "I'll be sure to celebrate with you too, soon. I wish I was there. I miss you already" she said to me in a little baby voice. "I have a few more important meetings I must follow up with or else your ass would be mine!" she said, more demanding. "No. Your ass would be Mine, I said matter-of-factly. And she knew it.

I immediately thought of getting intimate. I remembered the touch of Olivia's extra soft golden caramel skin and her hypnotizing eyes. Then I remembered the homemade video she sent me months ago of her being seductive.

"I'll send you another sexy video of me baby" she said as if she could read my mind.

"I'll be looking forward to it" I said. "I hope it beats your last one. That's gonna be hard to top."

"Not so much", she said, as if she already had something in mind. In the last seductive video she sent me, she was wearing nothing more than a pair of purple open-toed stiletto heels while holding onto a purple tasseled hand whip. She would slowly caress the whip against herself while talking low and seductively to me, all while the camera moved up and down to showcase all the curves and sexiness she exhibited. I was disrupted in my thoughts when my phone lit up to show that Hoshi was ringing in."

"Hoshi is calling on the other line sweetheart, let me get this call. We are going to be doing some brainstorming for the setup for the next event. I'll be quite busy, so I'll call you later".

"Okay, I love you babe" she said, then I clicked my line over. "Are you ready to continue practicing on your new skill?" Hoshi asked me. "Yes sir, I am. There's something new I'm going to work on for Olivia and she's going to love it. I'll be in the lobby in ten so we can go over a few minor details as we discussed". He made a clicking sound then he hung up the phone. I threw on a grey vest and left my room as I took the elevator down 27 floors to the lobby. Hoshi sat by himself, sipping on a glass of champagne. I sat next to him and ordered a scotch dry.

For the next two hours I listened to Hoshi explain and critique several ideas on market expansion and mind control. My favorite topic to listen to Hoshi speak on was mind control. He taught me that controlling your mind is the key to anything you want in this world, and once you conquer it then you can do anything. He would get deep and always spoke with passion about what he loved and believed in. I got a lot of passion from the words he spoke and some of the things he would do. Hoshi was a friend that touched me deeply, physically, mentally, and emotionally and I was able to pass that on.

CHAPTER 3

I'm so happy I was able to get that deal today!" I said with much excitement to Ava.

"I'm so happy and proud of you" Ava said. "I know! It really wasn't as hard or frightening as I made myself so anxious about it being. Seeing that they were hounding me like a juicy steak, I knew I would be okay when I got back into their office. These two middle eastern dudes were all over me. I can't tell if they signed because they needed my services or just to get me to come back again!".

"Whatever it was, it got you the deal girl" Ava said.

"Absolutely. I wish Kane was here to help me celebrate but it's okay. I've got a surprise for him when I see him and speaking of seeing him, I'm thinking of getting a ticket to Paris to go see my love. It's such the perfect time and place".

"I thought you had another meeting?" Ava asked.

"I do, but technically it's something I'll be doing primarily online so I don't necessarily have to be here. I actually told Kane I would be here longer so that I *could* surprise him" I explained to her.

"Let's go out for a few drinks and some dancing so you can help me figure out my next move".

"Okay honey. Where are we hitting up tonight?" she asked. I paused then said, "Kane's took me to a few places I like in the uptown area. I know we can find something out there, but I do have one spot in mind. It's called The Maze and they make some great cocktails.

"Hell yeah!" she shouted, "I went there last week with my boo Justin and it was lovely inside. Justin even knows the DJ and one of the managers there. I'll make sure we have a great time tonight." When she said that, I knew I was going to enjoy my night with Ava.

"Pick me up around 10. That gives you about two and a half hours to get ready, so don't keep me waiting." I told her before hanging up.

I wanted to look sexy but sophisticated, so I wore a red mid-length cross back dress with red five-inch Jimmy Choo heels. Ava wore a red skirt with a halter looking top that only covered her breasts. We were both stunning looking women and together we really turned heads. You would have thought we were celebrities. Sometimes that's exactly what I felt like.

About six men approached each of us on the way to our section. It's great to be beautiful but sometimes it gets annoying to hear each man that passes you say it.

There was already a set up of six vodka shots along with two specially made cocktails for each of us. We made cheers to my special day and to the good life and downed our shots of John Marc XO. The good mix of hip-hop and R&B the DJ played kept me and Ava hyped up most of the night until we sat down to rest our feet.

"Isn't that Lance, the sexiest and hottest producer and CEO of Get Hot Records?" Ava shrieked.

"I honestly don't even know what the man looks like, but he is some eye candy!" I said over my shoulder to her.

"I know I'm with Justin right now, but if I ever got the chance, I sure would take it. I love me some J, but damn that man is something else"! She was in a small world of her own.

"I got what I want and then some" I said to Ava. "Kane's all I want and need".

She got up and turned to face me with a smile and started dancing and shaking her ass so that Lance could get a good look at what her mama gave her. I paid him no mind as I started dancing and shaking my ass with Ava. About two minutes later we both spun around as we heard a grown and sexy man's voice say, "Excuse me miss". It was Lance, along with five of his goons standing behind us. He grinned and showcased a smile that reminded me of Kane's. He sure was a lot more attractive up close and in the light.

"My name is Lance and I see you two beautiful ladies over here alone. I won't intrude but I will let you know that my section is right next door so feel free to visit".

He looked at me and winked. Ava couldn't get her jaw off the floor fast enough to say anything before he left, and it was probably best she didn't. For the rest of the night Lance had rounds of shots and drinks sent to our table but we barely touched half of them. By the end of the night we were going to need to Uber home.

"If you two ladies are too over the top to drive, I'll be glad to have my chauffeur take you both home. Just let me know whatever you like." It seemed like Lance was trying to come on a bit sly and strong, but it could have been him sincerely just looking out for our safety. Ava spoke before she had time to think. "We would absolutely love to take your offer, wouldn't we Ava?" she said, slurring half of her sentence. "I certainly can't drive us, and neither can you. You can take me home Lance" she said, batting her eyes. "I will be more than glad to" he said, never taking his eyes off of me. Since I was not about to drive Ava's car or let her leave without me, I accepted his offer. Lance is a top-notch materialistic type of guy, so it wasn't a surprise when his chauffeur had whipped around in an all white Lamborghini limo. It was something exquisite and unique with all the bells and whistles. We listened to his tracks while Ava danced along before he burst into conversation. "What do you think about that sexy?" Lance gestured towards me, showing his white teeth.

"Music isn't really my specialty but I think they aren't bad" I said.

"I think they are *jamming*!" Ava said from the other side of me. He pulled out a business card and slid it between my fingers.

"You should give me a call sometime. I have a business opportunity that could work for you" he said, loud and proud. As we pulled up in front of Ava's house we were helped out by his overweight chauffeur. Lance leaned his head halfway out the window licking his plump pink lips and thanked us for the company and told us to have a good night and morning.

Ava poked at me in envy knowing that Lance was mostly feeling me tonight. "If you're not going to use that card, I will!" she said "Don't lose it". I had no intentions of giving Lance a call, but I was going to keep the card anyways.

As we joked around about how many drinks he had sent us and how amazing our night had turned out to be, we both still ended up falling asleep with another glass of wine in our hands.

CHAPTER 4

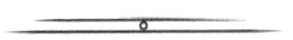

I stroked the brush across the canvas running a red curve from one end to the other. I glided my fingers between the paint to blend and swirl three bright colors together giving me a vibrant hue. Hoshi stood across the room from me examining his own work. He wasn't working on anything in particular but I knew it would be something meaningful. I swiped the flat bristles up and to the left giving the figure I had painted a fine look. I wasn't sure what the final outcome of what I was going for, so I took a small break to clear my mind. I began to unbutton my painted overalls as I drifted by Hoshi and headed for the restrooms to wash my hands and face.

I stood in front of the mirror with the water dripping off my face onto my chest, cooling my body. I stood there for five minutes thinking about the tension inside me and how good it would be to release myself. I watched that area of my pants begin to stick out as I rubbed my hand on it from the outside, picturing Olivia's ass spread in front of me. I unzipped my zipper and watched my master stick out and stand tall. I looked at my piece with a smile knowing how much satisfaction it provided. I stood sideways by the mirror while I massaged around the tip slowly making circular twisting motions with my hand. I whispered Olivia's name as I continued with my imaginative fantasy. I suddenly stopped when I heard a noise come from behind the bathroom door. I was so in the moment of feeling myself that I didn't notice Hoshi had poked his head in to make sure I was okay. I calmed myself down and got myself together so I could think about what I would do next. I wiped myself with a warm rag and left the bathroom to head back to the studio area.

When I got to my space, I asked Hoshi if everything was okay and if he needed anything from me. There wasn't an awkward moment when we looked at each other because we are comfortable together and in our own skin. He said I had left in such a hurry and that he was just checking to see if everything was alright with me since he didn't get a response when he called my name a few times before coming to look for me.

I sat in front of my painting wondering about Olivia, my next brush selection and releasing the built-up tension still inside me. I fell back into seeing explicit images and sensing the touch of her mouth on me. I began to bulge some more so I slightly turned myself and slipped my erect cock outside my pants. I licked my lips as I felt my shaft throb and my balls tingle. I felt that Olivia was thinking about me that same moment. I closed my eyes and slowly stroked my dick between my hands. I couldn't and didn't want to stop what I had started so I made myself comfortable and continued. Before I could open my eyes, Hoshi had come and placed his hand on my back. "I see someone is a bit excited and can't hold it in" he said, staring at my hard dick. My dick was so hard I could feel my veins pulsating out of it. He had startled me at first, but I got back into my groove not caring he was right there. I closed my eyes again to envision her mouth around me. I felt Hoshi move away from me. I slowly thrusted my pelvic area upwards as I felt the change in pace and feeling. I stood up and looked down at my distraction as I began to stroke some more.

CHAPTER 5

I woke up this morning excited, ready to go to Paris and with Kane on my mind. I knew he was planning ahead and was up to something before he left for France and I wanted to surprise him with a plan of my own.

Kane had been so romantic and helpful these past few weeks that I decided to blow his mind one night with me and these two Brazilian twins that I came across while in my yoga trapeze class. We became text friends then gradually started hanging out before and after our classes. They were both great gymnasts and showed me a few stretches that even Kane loved to see me in. It may sound a bit strange to let him be with another female, let alone twins, but I never felt happier and more content in our relationship. I knew this would definitely beat any homemade video clip I could send him. It would be the first time he's done anything like this before and I wanted to take his virginity.

Juliana, Adriana and I had met 30 minutes before our last class, so I took that opportunity to share my idea with them. They both accepted in exchange for 2k apiece and first-class flights. I was glad they accepted and was even more anxious to see how everything would turn out. They were going to fly in the following day then we would all part ways that night. I gave them half of their payment upfront and would give the other half once the night was over. I sent a text over to Adriana and Juliana to let them know that I would be taking my flight soon and that I would keep in touch if anything were to change. I called Ava over to have her help me with my packing. I had barely mentioned the twin idea to her, but she made sure to get her opinions out there. "So, are you sure you're ready to do this?" she asked me. "It'll change things a little, so I just hope he's a good guy. I remember when I offered to bring a female in with Justin. Afterwards he wouldn't stop asking me when we would do it again and how much fun he thought I was for doing it and blah blah. It was something he would always hint at almost every time we got intimate for the next two months. Yes, it was fun, but it had me feeling left out after-the-fact" she said disappointed. "I know Kane isn't Justin, but they are both men!" It wasn't anything I wanted to hear right before I put my plan into action, but it was well needed and appreciated words from a good friend.

I was excited myself for the experience so the thought of it didn't bother me much. "I know you will enjoy your trip so just hurry back and tell me all the details! In fact, you should record it".

"That's definitely being considered. I would like to sit back and watch that over again. I can't wait to see the look on Kane's face"

"I'll watch it with you freak, nasty" Ava said. "You're a freak too!" I said back to her.

I sat back in my seat clicking away at my phone screen playing the ancient game of Tetris before take off. I already knew exactly where to find Kane which was great for my surprise. I would pop up out of nowhere and surprise him. I'm not big on pop up surprises but I had to give it a try. I packed lightly knowing that I would only be there for no more than 48 hours before I was headed back home. I wore half of my clothing on the flight. I had worn a red teddy with a red garter belt under a red silk satin robe dress with red heels to play with his mind. I wanted to play with my mind before I got to Kane, so I got up from my seat, found my way to the bathroom and locked myself in. The bathroom on the jet is very spacious so I had room to sit on the toilet as I spread my legs across the counter. I looked at my spread lips in the mirror across from me and touched them lightly. I licked my fingers as I went on to make circular motions on my pressure points. My pussy got wetter as I watched myself squirt a little over the seat. I pulled my legs back some more as I caressed my juices slightly outside my hole. I could feel my pussy muscles contracting. I squeezed in and out trying to reach a quick orgasm. I wet my fingers again and pressed on my throbbing clitoris as I squirted all over the mirror and floor while watching some of my cum slide down my ass. I licked my lips in fulfillment and let the remains of my cum drip into the toilet as I wiped myself down. That was a great pre- tease to get me ready for Kane when I saw him. I freshened up and went back to my seat to read up on some news and to make a few calls before my arrival. There would be no time for talking once I made my entrance.

I pulled in front of La Maître with all eyes on me. I was a beauty and Paris was the perfect place for me to be. I walked in and went to the front desk and asked the attendant who was eyeing me up and down if a Kane Evans was staying at this hotel. He politely replied with a smile that they weren't able to give out that information. But for a price you can get and find whatever you need. I slid him $200 for a room number and a card. I was ready to pounce on Kane, so I anxiously took myself up twenty-seven floors and to the left to his suite. I opened the door and walked around his room to find it quiet and empty. I figured Kane must have been down the courtyard in his studio working on his artwork or having an important talk with an associate. I was a bit afraid of ruining anything he had going on at the time that I would be walking in, but I was going to make it all worth it. I made my way to the studio arts building where Kane's work area occupied a large space. I pranced myself up the stairs inching my way closer to him. I stopped in front of the door and took a deep breath. I slowly opened the door hoping he wouldn't hear or see me enter if he were inside. As I closed the door, I faintly heard a noise, but I couldn't hear who it came from or what was said. I quietly turned my phone recorder on and slowly walked in and looked around the wall to surprise my baby.

To my great surprise I did not walk in to see Kane working on a masterpiece of art, instead I stumbled in to see Hoshi on his knees gagging on about 8 inches of Kane's cock. I froze in shock and amazement. Before either one of them realized they had been walked in on, I quickly turned around and shut the door. I stood outside the hallway in paralysis as so many thoughts ran through my head.

Do I go back in and expose them? Do I act like I didn't just witness my man getting his dick choked on by his mentor? Then I thought about the twins and my own surprise. I was okay with the thought of two females fucking on my guy so was it right for me to get upset because he chose a guy instead? Besides the fact that I caught him doing something behind my back. Was it any better to let two girls do the same thing? I guess in so many ways it is, but I didn't know what to think or what to do. I walked out the building and into the courtyard to get some air as I looked through my phone to call Ava.

Should I leave... should I say something, or maybe I should even join them? What am I going to do?

The Hard Part

CHAPTER 1

I pulled in towards the entrance of the condo building, parking my Audi right in the front. I looked at the clock, which read 11:58 a.m. I was just in time for my appointment. I eased my way through the small crowd to the lobby and into the elevator. I pressed the button for the ninth floor and felt the elevator go up. Once the doors opened, I walked out and started to unbutton my shirt halfway down to my bra. When I reached the door, I knocked three times then another two before I opened the door and walked in. I sat on the sectional facing the kitchen waiting for him to appear. I waited for three minutes before I saw his wet glistening body come around the corner and head in my direction. I wasted no time getting to work on him. He stood in front of me naked as I slapped the head of his dick across my lips while I slowly let my tongue hover over his oozing hole. I let my tongue drip with saliva as I licked the top of his shaft down to his balls. I took my shirt off and laid down on the couch, feeling the cool leather on my back as he stood over me and started to teabag me. Since he knows I'm a sucker for pain, he wrapped his hands around my neck while he forced his dick in and out of my mouth. I let him face fuck me while I touched myself. "Damn girl, that shit feels so fucking good" he said to me in complete bliss with his eyes closed. I was about to take him to another world in a few minutes. He slowed his strokes while he watched me from the side, pulling my hair back so he could enjoy the view. "It's coming baby". He went a bit faster and harder, hitting the back of my throat each time till he finally came down my esophagus. He grunted and shook his legs, jumping up and down as if he just scored a touchdown. I got up and went to the bathroom to clean off my face and to hop in the shower before I left to go have some lunch. "I love that pretty little mouth of yours. I'll be sure to have a surprise for you next time" he said to me from behind the door. "Better hurry up or you'll be late for your lunch" he said sarcastically. I glammed myself up before exiting the bathroom and started towards the kitchen to grab me a bottle of water. "It sure was nice to see you this morning, can't wait to see you again" he said, while slapping me on my ass. He turned to give me a soft kiss on the cheek then Lance disappeared around the corner and into his den.

: : :

"What do you mean they're not going to honor their half of the contract?" Kane said in anguish. "I see that's something I'll have to deal with them in court about, and you can tell them, I'll see them there" Kane said aloud before hanging up the phone. "I can't believe the shit they're trying to pull on me" he said looking through his phone and shaking his head in disappointment. I had done some commercial construction and architectural work for a company that did not disclose that they were on the verge of going bankrupt and was not sure they would honor the other half of the contract. I was sure to lose at least half a million dollars, if funds could not be recovered for my work per the contract. I was outraged because of the time and money spent and because of all the extra headaches I'd have to go through. I punched in my legal adviser's number to consult with them on the issue. They would make this all run smoothly and keep it uncomplicated. Losing money in business is never a good thing, but it always reminds me not to get too comfortable with people even when you think everything is great.

I tapped my pen on the edge of my cherrywood desk, thinking about how soon I could bounce back from this unfortunate setback. It really did not set me back financially, but it was a loss I wanted to recover for my own sake. That would have to be put on hold until after I met with Olivia for a late lunch. I called The Matrix to set up reservations for Olivia and myself before I left my office. I jotted down some ideas and numbers I would need for a later project before sliding out of my office chair and into my Porsche seat. I revved the engine and took off onto the Interstate, putting my windows down and turning my music up. I raced my way alongside a Mercedes e400 till I took my exit and maneuvered into the parking lot. I sprayed two pumps of cologne on my neck and chest and straightened my collar and cuffs before I entered the building to sit and enjoy lunch with my wife.

CHAPTER 2

I sat at the table eyeing the couple next to me trying to figure out what their conversation was all about. The lady at the table looked displeased with her date and had a confused expression on her face. I felt like I could understand her thoughts and feelings. I looked to the front of the restaurant where I saw Kane speaking with the host. I stood up and smiled when we locked eyes as he made his way to the table. Kane stood in front of me kissing me lightly on my cheek. "You smell amazing and look stunning, as always" he said with his killer smile.

Kane and I got married ten months ago, but I never brought up the incident I came across that day in Paris. I didn't know how to confront him anymore. My feelings got the best of me that night and I left Paris, canceling my plans and crying myself to sleep on the flight home. I couldn't stand to be alone once I had returned home. I called Ava to see if she could console me, but she was knocked out cold, so I ended up pulling out my card case and flipped through them till I came across the one Lance had slid between my fingers. I needed to open up and express my feelings to someone who I thought could be understanding and a good listener. His company was better than I intended. Lance listened to me thoroughly and patiently as I vented about what to do and how I felt. He never pushed up on me, which I thought he was sure to do, and that instantly made me feel more comfortable being around him. I didn't want to forget about my love for Kane, but I made a friend in the process of this mistake and it wasn't the only thing I would get out of it. I watched Kane's lips move as I thought about how sexy both men were. I felt like anytime I was with

Lance, I thought of Kane, and now being around Kane had me thinking about Lance. I did not have strong feelings for Lance, but he was starting to crowd my brain a bit too often lately.

Kane went on to tell me about a small battle he was about to face with a company that he would be taking to court over an unfinished contract. It frightened me a bit to see the rage in his eyes as he spoke. He never lost his cool and rarely got out of line when issues would arise, but this seemed to have pressed a hard button within him. "It's all going to be okay sweetheart, trust me" I said as I put my hand on top of his. "Let's just enjoy our lunch now, then later you can get down to the bottom of it. What are you ordering today?" I asked, trying to change the subject. Kane ordered the Lobster Thermidor with an extra side of grilled shrimp and I would feast on a sea scallop risotto alongside some stuffed calamari. Kane and I laughed and shared stories of our happiest and most embarrassing moments, letting our worries disappear. My embarrassing moment happened on my 21st birthday when Ava and I went to Vegas. I clearly had way too many drinks and thought I was okay and looking cute, until I face planted down six missed steps, exposing everything underneath my dress. I'm sure someone caught that on camera. Kane told me his moment happened one April fool's day in high school. A friend he had been paired with for a project embarrassed him by slipping in a five-second video clip of him dancing naked in front of a mirror, into their slideshow, that was shown to at least 30 students.

We poked fun at each other, smiling and enjoying each other's company till we finished our meals. "I really love the way you make me feel, Olivia" Kane said with passion. At that moment I forgot about everything. I wanted it all to go back to being too good to be true. I wanted Kane to be my one and only, but I went into such a rampage that now too much had happened, but I still loved my husband. I took Kane's hand and intertwined it with mine. I looked at him and blew him a kiss. He pulled my arm closer and kissed the top of my hand then stood up from the table. He pulled out my chair and walked me to the front of the restaurant. We stopped and mingled for a few minutes with another couple coming in to dine, that knew Kane, before we got into our vehicles and parted ways till we met later that night at home.

CHAPTER 3

I walked my way around Herman Park looking for a visible shaded area to sit and relax before my adviser could make it over to this side of town. I had changed into my workout gear and sat for 10 minutes to brainstorm on what I could possibly do with the property. Afterwards, I rented a bike and meandered around the park taking in the fresh air and cool breeze. Couples were having picnics; families were taking pictures beside the fountains and ducks waddled here and there searching for any loose bread they could find. I set my alarm to go off 15 minutes before my adviser would arrive giving me enough time to ride my bike back to its station. I cooled down and wiped the sweat off my face. I called Stanley to give him my exact location and less than two minutes later he found me. He got out of his car and walked my way carrying a briefcase and a backpack. He sat next to me tossing the backpack on his lap then unzipped it and pulled out a large laptop, turning it on and facing it towards me. Stanley explained the best choices for me to get the most out of my possible loss. I had several options to choose from and using it for my own purposes would not be the one I would choose. I could and possibly would choose to sell it to another company even though it was being custom built. Stanley's computer screen displayed pie charts and bar graphs alongside lots of other data that related to my business and finances. I sat back on the bench playing out each scenario and thinking of which choice would provide the best turnaround within six months. I grabbed the laptop and started scrolling to see everything on my own. Stanley opened his briefcase and started to go through a pile of papers. "You may want to look over these. You might find something else in there" he said, handing me a big stack of papers. "Take the briefcase and return it to me in court. I hope this helps a lot" he said, before getting up to leave. I nodded to him and began to sift through a few pages before stuffing them back into the briefcase. I got up and walked back to my car.

I was going to head back to my office to get a better look into the situation. I placed the briefcase on the passenger seat and zoomed away to Washington Street. I was stopped on the way in by my assistant who had informed me I had an important missed call from Titan, the company I would be seeing in court. I got to my office and called the President of Titan to see what he had to say. To my great surprise, I was stunned when he told me they would be going through with the contract and meeting them in court would not be necessary. I smiled with joy knowing things would go as originally planned. We finished our conversation with a scheduled appointment in three days and some general timeline Q & A's. I got off the phone in a better mood. I was still a bit anxious to look at the information in the briefcase, so I grabbed the handle and swung it across my desk. About 1500 papers were jam packed inside but nicely organized and sorted by subject with colored paper clips and paper holders. I started going through a stack that had multiple sticky notes attached to it. It was practically the same information he had already shown me earlier at the park. I scanned through the documents and set aside those with my financial records and other income receipts.

Before I got into sorting through everything, I made a call to Hoshi. I explained to him how the contract was still valid, and I wouldn't be needing much assistance since I would no longer be going to court. Hoshi was one of my lawyers and he was going to assist in this case as well. His many talents allowed him to do many things. "I'm glad this has been resolved the right way and without the extra headache" I said into the phone. "Yes, that is good, but it is not over yet" he said to me. "I advise that you look into your files a bit more to stay on top of it." Once he hung up, I zoned out and concentrated on the numbers in front of me. It was too much to go through, so I broke it down into sections starting on my personal finances then moving into my business finances. I feel it's better to have someone else handle my finances and other areas I'm not that savvy with. I choose to focus more on my stronger skills. That's what advisers are paid for. Looking through all the papers was going to take focus and I didn't have that much patience at the moment. As I scrolled down the left side of my statement, I noticed something was awkwardly out of balance. I rubbed my eyes and blinked fast as I continued to look through my financial records. There must have been some sort of mistake. Between the months of June and August my balance had drastically fluctuated, but nothing made sense to me. I had not made any transactions with this account in over a year. Again, I began to feel confused and enraged. I found the number to my personal financial assistant on my account. I called and it was explained to me that the funds had been transferred into another account. I stayed on the phone for almost two hours till I got to the bottom of this huge mistake.

CHAPTER 4

W hy are we here?" I asked Kane happily, as he laid down the red and white checkered blanket. He placed the basket down and set everything out for a cute surprise date. "I just wanted to take some time out to remind you of the man I am" he said with a smirk as he popped open the bottle of wine and poured our glasses. "I'll never forget the handsome and courageous man I married" I said. "So how is everything going with your promotions, fundraisers, and of course that bump in the road you came across?" I asked with concern. "It's been going extremely well, and I wouldn't want it going any other way. Everything I came across that was a problem turned itself around. How is business on your end?" he asked in return. "Pretty good as well for me" I stated proudly. "I have thought about starting a new fashion apparel company. I have some great ideas and a few samples to show off as well as people already lined up to go to work for me". I took a sip of wine. "Ava will be helping me get everything started and will be sharing her ideas with me. She's not so bad herself in that field, plus she provides some great contacts. She just might be my business partner in this one" I said, envisioning the outcome I was expecting. "Well then, it sounds like you've got everything figured out there. How long have you been wanting to do this? How much research have you done into it?" he said intensely, sounding like a concerned parent. "I've done quite a bit of looking into the industry and speaking with a few owners to get a better understanding of it. There's a lot to learn but you only get true knowledge with experience, so I'm thinking that within four months' time, Ava and I can come up with a master plan to execute. I think I want the company name to be K.O. but who knows what Ava will think about it." "Interesting name" he said between his bites of cheese and crackers. "What else has been going on with you, honey?" he asked as if he were waiting for me to give him a specific answer. "Besides that, I have also thought about the idea of producing my own fragrance. They sort of go hand-in-hand. I have spoken with experts and I have a great sense of smell. It will be so exciting. I visualize myself as chairwoman and CEO of a large corporation. I grinned from ear-to-ear.

"My downline for the online gig has grown substantially since putting in that extra SEO work you advised me to do with your friend Sam. Thanks for all the help you gave me," I said leaning over to give him a kiss but he slightly turned his head and took a gulp of wine. "Oh, of course you're welcome for the help I gave you. Are you going to thank me for the help I *didn't* give you?" he said with slight attitude, making me a bit confused. "What do you mean?" I asked, raising my eyebrows. "Explain?" I said, as a question. "I gladly will" he said sitting up straight. "Well it seems that one little bump in the road I came across didn't actually turn itself around. In fact, it's done nothing but make me furious and wonder what's going on in my life" he said a bit disappointed. "Okay..." I said, waiting for him to get to his point. "Do you want to explain to me why 1.2 million dollars is missing out of one of my accounts I did not give you access to"? My heart stopped and my mouth slightly opened. I immediately began to shake with anxiety. I had no clue what to say in the moment, even though I had certainly thought about how to explain my actions if this day were to ever come. In my dreadful moments of deceit against Kane, guilt never slipped my mind or feelings but during the moment of confrontation I felt awful, scared, and wanted to take it all back but was then reminded of the images that fueled my own outrage. Maybe I did go a bit overboard but there was no turning back now. I looked back at Kane and smiled then picked up the bottle and downed the rest of the wine.

The Last Part

Till death do us part. Those were some of the precious words I spoke aloud to my wife not even a year ago and I was already considering thoughts of divorce in my head. I couldn't believe the chain of events that were playing out. How and why could she do something like this to me and where was the money she took? I've been robbed and stolen from before but never with this kind of pain attached to it. The dollar amount hurt me a bit, but I was more shocked to know she would do such a thing. I couldn't help but think about how amazing things had always seemed to be. What happened and where did I go wrong? I tried to keep my cool as long as I could but thinking of Olivia taking that amount of money from me, made me furious. I had been happy and willing to help her with anything she wanted to do so why would she deceive me like this? I couldn't think of anything that would make her act out this way and there was no excuse good enough for an action so devious. I flashed through the good times we had but I became numb to the thought of her devilish behavior. What else was she capable of doing to me? I did not care to find out and I did not care to extend any sympathy. At the end of the day, she took something from me that I worked hard for and was precious to me as much as she was. Divorce and restitution were the end result I thought about most. As I glared at Olivia, I could only think about a few things I wanted to do to her, but I held myself in check. I would take her down where it hurts. "Out of all the people in my life to do this to me, why you Olivia? Why this?" I placed my hand on my head as I paced back and forth in front of her. "What the fuck were you thinking, huh? Are you stupid or something?" I screamed at her, making her head spin. I went on with my tantrum for a few minutes then I turned around and froze.

My head was spinning, and my stomach felt nauseous. Never did I think I would find myself in a situation like this. The fury in his tone and body language instantly changed the mood. I was being backed into a corner and this was a fight I was certainly not prepared for but wasn't willing to lose. I jumped up and tried to calm him down, but he only went on with his cursing tantrum. A way I've never seen Kane act. "I'm Pregnant!" I finally shouted to him. He stopped and looked at me with confusion but quickly went back to being unsympathetic towards me. The news of him potentially being a father didn't phase him at all. Part of me was angry with him about it but another part of me felt bad for him. Deep down, I was not sure if Kane or Lance was the father of my child. I had taken a test nine days ago when I vomited twice for no reason after eating breakfast. The feeling of excitement and worry all flooded over me at the same time but I wouldn't reveal that to him. Kane didn't seem to care about anything anymore. He paced back and forth in front of me throwing profanity words towards me. I finally had enough of him acting like he was the perfect one in the relationship. I picked up my phone and scrolled to what I was looking for. As he came towards me with his loud outrageous outbursts, I turned my phone towards him, so he was able to see himself stroking his dick in and out of Hoshi's mouth. He turned white and froze in shock. Kane turned so pale it was as if his inner ghost was displaying itself in front of me. "Is this the new image you want people to have of you?" I asked him. If having his baby wasn't going to calm him down, then I knew this would do something. Blackmailing my way out was not the route I wanted to take but it had just drastically turned to that. But would I really do that? Would Kane really divorce or sue me and file criminal charges? At this point, everything went from being too good to be true to too bad to be real.

To be continued...